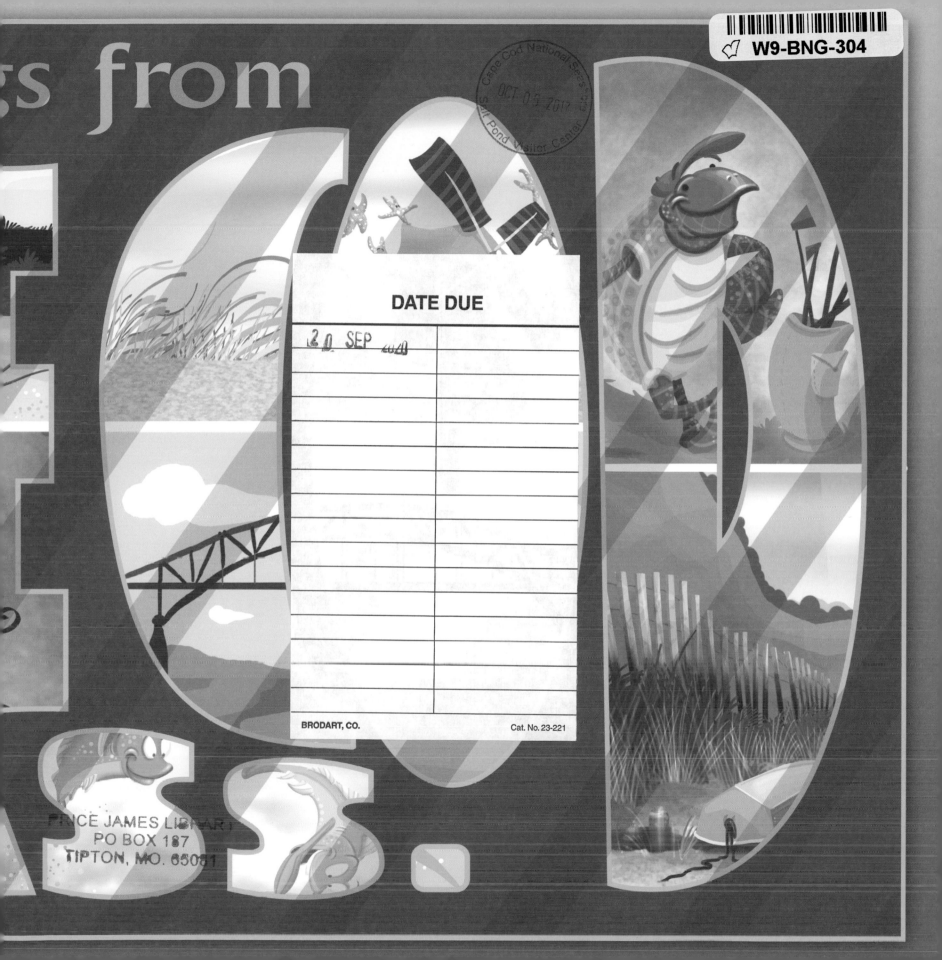

ISBN 978-1-933212-78-4

Designed by John Barnett/4 Eyes Design

Printed in China

Published by Commonwealth Editions, an imprint of Applewood Books, Inc.,
P.O. Box 27, Carlisle, Massachusetts 01741
Visit us on the Web at www.commonwealtheditions.com.

10 9 8 7 6

The Cods of Cape Cod

Love their Summer Vacation

BY ED SHANKMAN

ILLUSTRATED BY DAVE O'NEILL

Commonwealth Editions
Carlisle, Massachusetts

The Cods of Cape Cod
Love their summer vacation,
And though they could go
Anywhere in the nation,

They keep coming back
To their favorite location,
'Cause they know Cape Cod's
A vacation sensation!

The Cods of Cape Cod
Have a house on the beach,
And it's just the right size,
With a fish tank for each.

They love that old house,
Every board, every stone,
And there's nothing like fish
With a home of their own!

HOME
SWEET
HOME

The Cods never know
Who they'll see by the sea,
'Cause their friends come to visit
Whenever they're free.

Those sea creatures wake up
Before the first rooster
To travel from Truro
And Yarmouth and Brewster.

Some sail from Woods Hole,
And some walk from Orleans,
Wearing flip-flops and tank tops
And old cut-off jeans . . .

From Provincetown too,
And Hyannis and Dennis,
For miniature golf
Or a few games of tennis.

The shrimp comes from Sandwich,

The bass from Mashpee,

And the swordfish from Chatham
By way of the sea.

The crabs and the clams
Come together by car,

And the whale finds his way
By the light of a star.

The sharks and the stripers
Bring haddocks and pipers
And one baby bluefish
In bright colored diapers.

They breeze by the windmill,

They slosh through the bog,

They flash by the lighthouse
That shines through the fog.

The cute and the fearsome,
The meek and the odd,
They all come to visit
The Cods of Cape Cod.

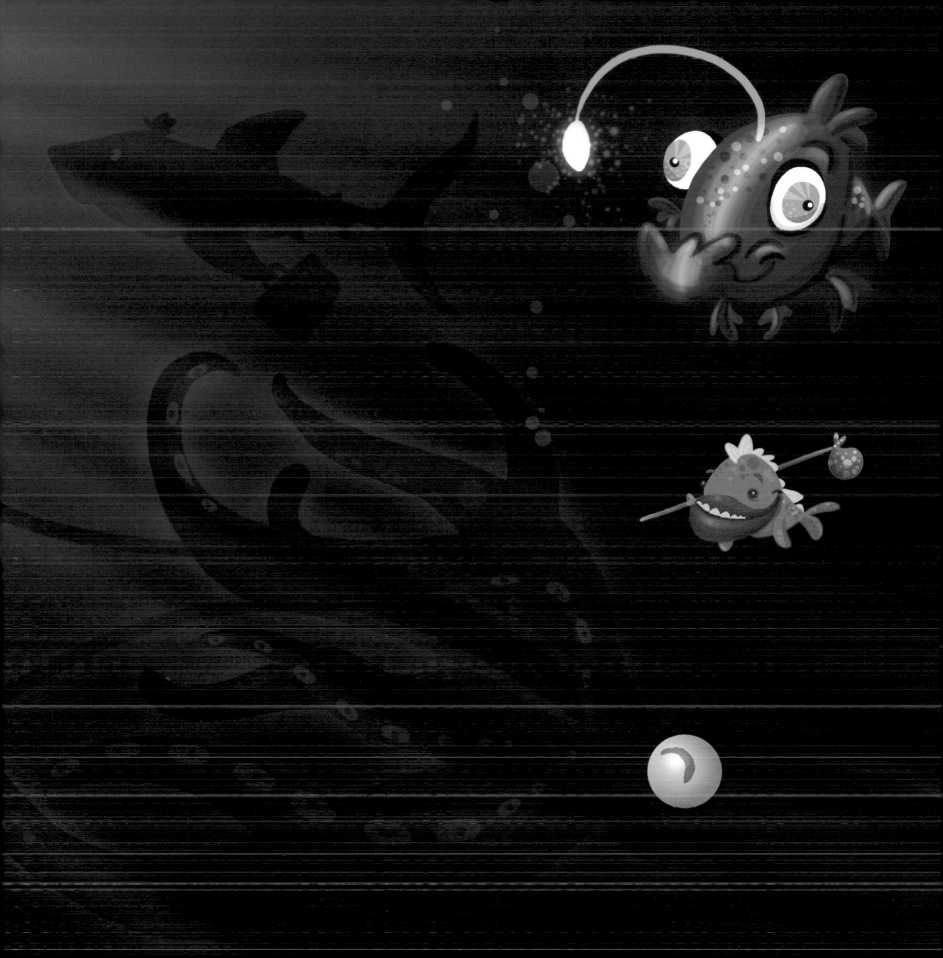

They come to the Cods
'Cause they want to have fun,
And when fun's what you want,
Cods are second to none!

They have fun in the sea.
They have fun in the sun.
They have fun on the sand.
They have fun on the run.

It could be at nine
Or a quarter past one—
When your host is a codfish,
The fun's never done!

Oh, they may stop their motion
To put on some lotion
Or gaze in a daze
At the waves of the ocean,

But two seconds later,
They're back in the bustle.
They're off like a missile
And ready to hustle.

You've heard they can swim?
Well, those stories are true.
There is no one who swims
Like the sea creatures do.

They wiggle and dart
With the greatest of ease,

Or they drift through a wave
Like a bird on a breeze.

They're completely relaxed,
So at ease with the seas,
That they easily manage
Whatever they please!

Their strokes are superb,
And their kicks are sublime,
And the lobster does two
Different strokes at a time.

When it comes to the water,
They do as they wish,
And if you can do that,
Then you may be a fish!

When the last swim is swum
And they're back on dry land,
The Cods and their friends
Set their sights on the sand.

First they scoop it all up
And they squeeze it just so,
Then they squish it as tight
As they think it will go.

And you know, if you've ever
Squished sand in your hand,
That it's almost more fun
Than a person can stand!

It is fun, that is true,
But the Cods aren't through,
'Cause when sand is at hand
There is much more to do.

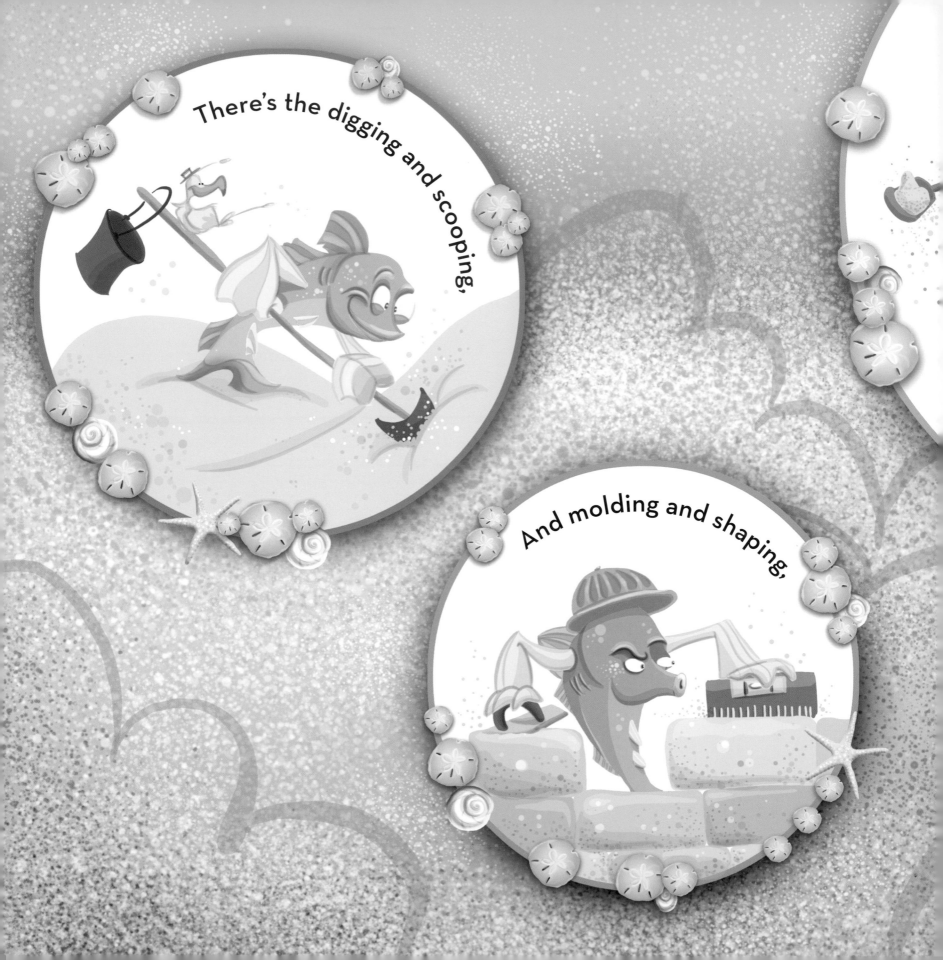

There's the digging and scooping,

And molding and shaping,

And building and rubbing,

And carving and scraping.

And then, in the end,
When the last sand is scooped,
And the last shape is scraped,
And the creatures are pooped,

Behold, it's a castle!
Just look at that thing!
Why, except for the sand,
That thing's fit for a king!

The design is exquisite!
Such taste! Such detail!
No one's ever done more
With a shovel and pail.

Then as day turns to night,
What the Cods like the most,
Is an old-fashioned, New England
Marshmallow roast.

And there's one thing for sure,
Though the Cods will not boast:
There's no question they host
The best roast on the coast!

First they toast every bite
'Til it's roasted just right,
And they savor each morsel
With all of their might.

Then they get up and dance
By the fiery light.
(And you'll never forget
That particular sight.)

Well, they've done it again.
What a great summer season!
The Cods of Cape Cod
Have had fun beyond reason.

If summer was something
A person could measure,
This could be the best
In the history of pleasure.

I know what you're thinking:
Yes, summertime ends,
And the Cods of Cape Cod
Must take leave of their friends.

But I'll tell you a secret,
Between me and you,
Summer always comes back . . .

. . . And the Cods come back too!

ALSO BY ED SHANKMAN AND DAVE O'NEILL

When a Lobster Buys a Bathrobe
My Grandma Lives in Florida
The Boston Baloonies
I Met a Moose in Maine One Day
Champ and Me by the Maple Tree
The Bourbon Street Band is Back

ALSO BY END SHANKMAN, WITH DAVE FRANK

I Went to the Party in Kalamazoo

ED SHANKMAN was born in the Bronx, New York, and lives today in Verona, New Jersey. As a creative director in the advertising industry, he has directed creative efforts for some of the world's best-known companies. Beyond the office, he has always spent his time chasing creative inspiration as a writer, guitar player, and painter.

DAVE O'NEILL has worked as a graphic designer and illustrator since receiving his bachelor of fine arts degree from William Paterson University in 2001. A native of Mount Olive, New Jersey, he now hangs his hat and sharpens his pencils in Montclair.

Greetin